AF449336

DELINA VASILIADI

PLAYING WITH ALICE

Translated from Greek to English

by Penny Fylaktaki

Pharos Books

ISBN: 978-93-55461-62-9
eISBN: 978-93-55461-78-0

© Publishers

Publisher: Pharos Books (P) Ltd.
Plot No.-55, Main Mother Dairy Road
Pandav Nagar, East Delhi-110092 (India)
Phone: +014049995474
WhatsApp: +014049995474
E-mail: sales@pharosbooks.in
Website: www.pharosbooks.in
Edition: 2022

PLAYING WITH ALICE
Author: Delina Vasiliadi

2018
First Prize
Greek Authors' Association

2018
Commendation
Panhellenic Authors' Association

2020
First Prize
"Book-Play of the year 2019"
Literary magazine Kefalos

2020
The play was included at the
"Books of the year 2019" list
Hellenic Cultural Association of
Greek Cypriots

ACT ONE

A messy space. Filthy. Full of dust. Furniture piled in total disorder one on top of the other or next to one another. Among the pieces of furniture are also some antiques of great value, such as a huge wooden trunk. The most prominent item in the room is a big set of drawers. Many papers and books are on it together with pens, pencils, quills and inkpots, an old lamp that hardly sheds any light, a half-empty glass of water, as well as a phone with an answering machine. Torn pieces of paper are scattered everywhere: on the floor, on the desk, on the furniture. A broken typewriter has fallen on the floor. A man enters. He holds papers in his hands.

MARK: (He tears them up and lets the pieces fall down. He writes.) A man walks in on the stage and sits on the chair. (MARK sits on a chair.) By the window. On stage? (He writes.) A man walks in the room and sits on a chair by the window. No. I don't remember this. A man. No. (He writes.) The man walks in the dark empty room and looks for a place to sit. It's always good to be looking for something, creates a sense of suspense. (He writes.) He looks for a place to sit. Finally, he sits on a chair by the open window. It's cold. No, it's not. The window is closed. So, it's hot. The man is sweating. Note: don't forget this later. (He writes.) The man. He sits on a chair by the closed window. He's waiting. Waiting. Waiting. Waiting... and then waiting some more... What is he waiting for? He waits for her. He waits for her who is gone for good. Who will never return. Won't return. Ever. No - too slushy. Far too slushy. Even for her. (MARK tears up the paper, throws it down on the floor together with the rest.) We need something more drastic here, more action... The man is waiting. (Phone ringing.) He is waiting for her... (Phone ringing.) He is waiting for her... (Phone ringing.) I won't have any work done today. They won't let me! (Phone ringing. MARK checks the incoming number. He won't answer. The answering machine starts.)

ANSWERING MACHINE: You have reached Mark and Alice Johnson. We are not here right now. Please leave your message and we'll get back to you as soon as possible. BEEP.

WOMAN'S VOICE: Mr. Johnson, it's Fanny, the secretary of Mr. Adams, your publisher. I'm calling to remind you that - (MARK finally rushes to pick up the phone.)

MARK: Yes? Speaking. I'm waiting. (MARK waits until they put him through to ADAMS.) Hello John. [...] Fine. Just great. [...] I'm telling you I'm ready. [...] I don't think you know who you're talking to. The work is finished. I can't see any reason for all these phone calls. [...] I'm not negotiating the deadline here. [...] I'm just working on the final draft. It's my best work. Until the next one, of course. Goodbye for now. (MARK puts down the phone.) Where was I? (MARK reads what he's written.) The man walks into the room and sits on a chair by the closed window. He's waiting. (Phone ringing. MARK won't answer. After five times, the answering machine starts.)

ANSWERING MACHINE: You have reached Mark and Alice Johnson. We are not here right now. Please leave your message and we'll get back to you as soon as possible. BEEP.

MAN'S VOICE: Good evening Mr. Johnson, this is Paul Mathews, from the newspaper "Art today." I have tried to reach you several times over the past few days. I'm calling because your interview will be out this Wednesday and you still haven't sent me the answers to my questions. Nor the photos. When you get this message, please call me back. Goodbye.

(MARK opens a drawer and searches. He opens another one and looks at the bookcase. He finally finds what he's looking for. It's a folded piece of paper. He unfolds it and reads.)

MARK: "Tell us some things about yourself. Your personal life and your journey in the world of art. How did you start? Where do you get your inspiration from? You're a multi-awarded writer. Tell us about your huge success and how this has affected your life. Tell us a few things about your previous works. Are you writing something new now? What are your dreams? What are you afraid of?" What I'm afraid of. I'm afraid that all this bullshit will make me miss the deadline. That's what I'm afraid of. (MARK folds the paper and puts it in his pocket. He starts writing again. Children's voices come in from the playground outside.) The man's waiting. He's waiting for her... (He writes.) While the voices of children can be heard from the outside. How can I possibly concentrate with all that noise? What have I done to deserve this? (He goes near the window and shouts out loud.) Why don't you get the hell out of here in that school of yours and get off my back? Thank God I never wanted any children. (MARK takes out of his pocket the interview sheet and sits at his desk to answer the questions. He drinks some water.) Question one: Tell us some things about yourself. Now what kind of a question is this? (He writes.) I was born in a small village. In the middle of nowhere, I should write. (He continues.) I grew up in nature, something which seriously affected my work. We used to get up before dawn to milk the cows and deliver the milk. I was that close to nature. Rolling in the mud all day long... Rolling with pigs... And that stench... You'd think it'd never come off. And then straight to school. (He writes.) My parents loved literature — my mother couldn't write her name, my father was an alcoholic. Always absent — and every evening we would read poetry and listen to classical music and talk about books and art, about the future that lay before me, cloudless and bright. What bullshit. Does anyone believe it, I wonder. (He writes.) At school I aced all my tests, of course. My parents didn't want to have an educated son, they'd rather have me roll in the muck and stink of goat cheese. (He writes.) Sitting in for the University entrance exams — in secret, of course! — was the only way out. Back in those hard times, my sole guide and consolation was Oscar Wilde's saying, "We are all in the gutter, but some of us are looking at the stars." I was one of those looking at the stars. Although I was deep in the... So many nights staying up late to study. I was stressed and worried my folks might get wind of me. I pretended to be asleep under my blanket and studied under a dim little light. I used to hide my books, lest anybody find them and discover what I was up to. But I was determined. I wouldn't stay in that godforsaken place any longer. No. I knew I had to leave. And I did. Never to return again. Ever. (Children's voices.) Not even when Alice asked me to show her all the places I grew up in. (He writes.) As soon as I entered the School of Philosophy, I did several jobs to make a living. Of course, my folks wouldn't send me any money. I had betrayed them. Instead of becoming a shepherd, I wanted to study. I wanted to be a writer. They had written me off. I had written them off first. I had come off their bog for good. (He writes.) As soon as I graduated, I got a full scholarship in Paris. There, I met a student at the School of Fine Arts, Alice, my wife. My inspiration and my muse. The love of my life. Too far-fetched. (He writes it off and tries again.) That's where I met Alice. My muse. The woman who stood by me throughout my life, through all my decisions. Much better. You were young. Beautiful. Ethereal, one might say. As if you walked a few meters above the ground. Your rich blonde hair fell on your shoulders. Such white skin. Such blue eyes. Your fingers. Long. Your crimson lips. You'd think Botticelli painted them. That was the first thing I ever told you. "Your lips, madam. I'm sure Botticelli painted them red." You laughed, I remember that. Of course, you did. What else would you do hearing such nonsense? (He writes.) We got married almost immediately. I was already writing poetry, novels and short stories, but it was then that I started writing plays. Plays, my ass. (Children's voices.) Quite often people asked us why we stayed childless. If it was a matter of choice or circumstance. The truth is, we didn't feel the need to have a family. Work, all kinds of errands, our life was so full it never dawned on us to have children. I guess I can now say we didn't want children, after all. Motherhood and fatherhood are not for everyone. I — we were... complete? No. Happy? I have to elaborate on this part later. (He writes.) Anyway, it was a joint decision, my wife's and mine. We saw eye to eye on this. Mmm. (He writes.) Note: Keep the "children" part short. (Children's voices.) Will you shut the fuck up? I'm trying to work here. (He writes.) When we came back to Greece, we settled in Athens. But our great love for Nature — yuck, I'll puke! — led us to live in the mountain. Somewhere far away from civilization, where I could find the peace and quiet I needed to throw myself into writing. Devotion. This sounds good. (He writes.) A good reason why we didn't have any children was because we wanted to devote myself to writing. Good. And we ended up in this shrine. Two years later, an entire suburb was built nearby. No more peace and quiet any longer. You chose it, remember? So that we could be together. So that nothing would distract us from our work. That's what you said. We didn't need any friends. Neighbors. Or social life. And I went along. So as not to lose you. To keep writing. You wanted absolute quiet when you were thinking. Creating. The truth is that here you wrote your best works. "The city of men without face," "White Island," "Storms," "The bronze deer." And then you got sick and it was all over. (He checks the question sheet.) Tell us about your previous works. (He writes.) As you all know, I have written novels, short stories and theatre plays. It is practically impossible to talk about the totality of my works. For this reason, I will focus on three plays only. "The City of Men without a face," "White Island" and "Storms." Your very best. Without a doubt. (He writes.) I will start from "White Island," which is the latest release. Besides, it was your favorite. I didn't find it so interesting, but you really believed in it. And of course you were right. (He writes.) I mainly write existential theatre –although I basically prefer comedies. Laughter. That's what we need. Don't take things so seriously. You didn't agree with me. Existential dramas and all this crap. Anyway. (He searches through his writings and reads the previous things he has written.) I mainly... (He writes.) "White Island" is no exception. As if it could be. (He writes.) It is about a person's identity quest. My heroes, Marius and Nicky, struggle to survive in a suffocating environment. And right there, through hardships and all, they realize who they really are. And what they want from one another. That's it. (He writes.) My play entitled "The city of men without a face" falls into the category of dreamy theatre plays. Or at least this is what the critics say. Four kids, creatures of a dreamy world, are in a cave and make no effort to come out. In there, they talk about their thoughts and dreams, their goals and desires as well as the love they feel and share with one another. Yet, the thought of going out never crosses their minds. They won't come out to see the world. You always wanted your heroes trapped, miserable, far away from the world. Misers. Suffering and not knowing it. Horrible. (He writes.) And finally, my play "Storms." A social play. Even though existential agony is on top of my concerns together with the fear of death, this is a story of love and lies. A very rich man, married without any children, lives the life of his dreams, when he is suddenly accused of being the father of a baby whose mother died at childbirth and revealed his name on her final breath. My hero denies all accusations and there starts his ordeal. It's not about proving his innocence or guilt, but handling the conflicts he has to go through. With his wife. His good-for-nothing brother. The baby's aunt, who started the whole thing. Enough. Let's get down to business. (MARK leaves the interview papers on a chair. He takes his play in his hands and reads.) The man is waiting. Waiting for her, who... Her who... The man is still waiting for her who... What did she call it? I can't remember. (MARK takes a piece of torn paper from the floor, reads it, tries to find the other pieces. He puts them all together on his desk and tries to complete the puzzle. He sits on the chair and starts writing again. This time on the torn papers.) The man is desperate and sits down again. No. This certainly wasn't it. (MARK gets up.) The man is desperate and starts pacing up and down. He then sits. Why will he sit again? (He looks at his own notes trying to make out the handwriting.) Fucking scribbles... Do not forget. He's also sweaty. It's hot. (MARK loosens his tie.) It's hot in here, too. (He writes.) The man is sweaty and roams the place. What is he looking for? He's looking for... Beats me. (Children's voices.) "Only the children know what they are looking for." Focus, Mark! On him! What is he looking for? He's looking for... What can a handsome, well-dressed, fifty-year-old man be searching for in a dark room with no furniture? If she were here, she'd tell me what to do. (He writes.) The man is frantically looking for whatever he's looking for, when suddenly he hears somebody calling his name. Before he can tell what's going on, a woman appears. (He writes.) The woman enters. Note: find a name for the woman. (He writes.) The man answers "You're late. Where have you been? Beats me. Where was she? Another note: Come up with where the woman was before her entrance in act one. (He writes.) Act Two. The man yells "Where are you?" in great despair. Nobody answers. For quite some time, there's silence. The man rises from his chair. Why was he sitting again? Note: Where is the hero at the end of act one? (He writes.) The man shouts out loud again "Where are you?"

ALICE (Off): Mark.

MARK: Who is it? (Enters ALICE.)

ALICE: There you are.

MARK: Alice? Is that you?

ALICE: Don't you recognize me? Have I changed so much?

MARK: At last! I've been thinking about you all the time.

ALICE: (Ironically.) Your prayers are answered.

MARK: Why did you leave me alone for so long?

ALICE: What are you doing alone in the dark?

MARK: Pardon?

ALICE: I said "What are you doing alone in the dark?"

MARK: (He writes.) The woman asks "What are you doing alone in the dark?"

ALICE: Well?

MARK: I'm writing a theatre play.

ALICE: Theatre again?

MARK: "We do not make theatre for its own sake. We do not make theatre to live. We make theatre to make ourselves richer, to make the audience richer and together to help create a wide, mentally rich and self-sustainable culture in our country." Koun said it.

ALICE: Just don't tell me you're still writing our play. (MARK nods.)You haven't finished it yet, have you? (PAUSE.) A little light might help. One, two, three. (The room is lit.) Now it will all come to light. (He looks around.) So, this is your hiding place.

MARK: What do you get out of this? You've always been a pain in the ass.

ALICE: Don't talk to me like that. You're hurting me. You know how sensitive I am. I can't think in the dark. This feeling of misery and closure in here makes me sad. (ALICE starts coughing.) How long has it been since anybody cleaned up this damp? (ALICE keeps coughing.) Open up a window, we'll choke on dust.

MARK: Everything bothers you. There we go again.

ALICE: Don't you shake a finger at me. Go open a window.

MARK: Have some water. (MARK offers ALICE the glass of water on the desk.)

ALICE: Let's get down to work. Clean up, tidy up, open the windows. Terrible. Such neglect.

MARK: What's with you and this house anyway?

ALICE: Nobody has been in here for ages. (ALICE steps on mud on the floor.) Gross. Mud. (ALICE takes off her shoe to clean it, leaves it on the floor and steps with naked feet on the broken parts of the typewriter. She moans with pain, bends down and picks up the piece. Her eyes are wet. She holds it like a baby.) My typewriter. It's broken. How? (PAUSE.) I asked you something.

MARK: I couldn't write. (ALICE picks up the rest of the typewriter parts from the floor.) I got furious and threw it down.

ALICE: I think we could fix it. (She places them carefully on a small table, stands for a while and looks at them. She tries to put the pieces together, as if making a 3D puzzle. She realizes there are pieces missing.) There are pieces missing. The letters are gone. (ALICE puts on her shoe and checks around. She picks up the torn pieces of paper from the floor. She reads.)

MARK: That's from the play.

ALICE: I can see. (MARK gets a paper and pen, ready to write.)

MARK: Well. We're behind time. Let's go. Let's write. (PAUSE.) I'm waiting.

ALICE: So am I.

MARK: What for?

ALICE: So far, you haven't even offered me a drink.

MARK: What drink?

ALICE: Anything with alcohol. A little drink. Or two.

MARK: Since when did you start drinking? (He doesn't wait for the answer.) No time for drinks. I have to finish this play. And I don't have any drinks.

ALICE: Do you mean you called me over to help you…?

MARK: But you are not.

ALICE: Why do you talk to me like that? I told you. I'm very sensitive! You called me over to help you, which I'll gladly do, and the help I'm about to give is like enormous, to say the least, and you still have nothing for me to drink? You've made no provisions? Unbelievable! Tell me what exactly you're trying to write.

MARK: I'm rewriting the story.

ALICE: Can you rewrite a story? (Children's voices. MARK checks his papers, while ALICE looks at him.) What are you doing now? Thinking? Again? Aren't you tired of thinking? All the time you think, think, think. And then write, write, write. And when someone talks about you, the first think they'll say is, "He's thinking all the time. And writing. Write and think!"

MARK: And what's the second thing they say?

ALICE: I see you still have the same pen.

MARK: When it's empty, I fill it up again.

ALICE: I thought you lost it. As if the earth opened up and swallowed it. Nice, ha?

MARK: Too poetic for my liking. You're not helping. I am more rational. My writing is... No beautifications. You know that. (PAUSE.)

ALICE: Well, I thought of a fantastic ending for your story. Your hero is alone, lonelier than ever before, he's lost it all. He's incapable of doing anything. He's finished. Life, career... He knows the deep shit-hole he's heading for. He falls down on his knees and asks for forgiveness, but forgiveness will never come. The end. What do you think?

MARK: Surely not the end I hoped for.

ALICE: It's not what we want, it's what we get. Still, I must confess you're pretty cool.

MARK: It's because I know I'm dreaming.

ALICE: Are you?

MARK: It's a strange feeling. As if I am talking to myself.

ALICE: Very poetic.

MARK: I can see you, hear your voice, smell your perfume. I can touch you. You're here. But still... I know I'm dreaming. "Believe in dreams, for in dreams the gate to eternity is hidden."

ALICE: Very inspired. Though I don't know how this will help you in your play. Still, very inspired. (PAUSE.) You look a little pale.

MARK: I'm fine.

ALICE: You're pale! And those clothes. They fall loose on you. You've lost weight. You haven't been eating well.

MARK: I've been eating splendidly.

ALICE: Fruit? Veggies? Fish? How's your vitamin D? Oh, you're not eating any gluten stuff, are you?

MARK: My diet is great, I already told you.

ALICE: Don't you raise your voice at me. You've lost weight. The woman says, "I've cooked some lentils."

MARK: (He writes.) The man says, "You know I hate lentils."

ALICE: "I love them. They are so nourishing."

MARK: "Why are we talking about lentils? I'm eating out."

ALICE: "I've been cooking all day. You'll eat whatever we have."

MARK: I don't like it.

ALICE: You're wrong. Lentils are super. I'm hungry. Is there anything in the fridge?

MARK: Nah.

ALICE: You mean no drink, no food, no nothing? A great host.

MARK: I'm not a host.

ALICE: You called me over. You have to take care of me.

MARK: "Woe to those who're hungry and hope for charity."

ALICE: There go old sayings! (She looks into her handbag.) I wonder if I have something to eat. I remember I had a bar of chocolate somewhere here... (ALICE finds the chocolate.) Voilà. No. Just the wrapping.

MARK: Are we going to get down to work? I'm running out of patience.

ALICE: No pressure. I can't take pressure. What have you written?

MARK: "The man, all sweat, is looking for..." I don't know what.

ALICE: Never mind. We'll figure it out later. Try to move on, for now. "The man was looking for... when suddenly..."

MARK: The man keeps looking for it, when he's violently interrupted by the sudden appearance of a lady.

ALICE: Perfect.

MARK: I'm back in shape. (He writes.) Of a lady.

ALICE: An unidentified lady. There has to be some mystery. Some... suspense, get it?

MARK: Get it. It'll be a hit. (He writes.) The man keeps looking for it, when he's violently interrupted by the sudden appearance of an unidentified lady.

ALICE: Elegant, smart, stylish. Pale as death. The darkness suddenly turns into a bright light and everything starts making sense, acquiring shape and voice... Truths come out, truths long lost in the dark.

MARK: Now you spoiled it again. Far too sappy. If you can't help, don't speak. (He writes.) The man says, "Where have you been?"

ALICE: The woman says, "Am I late?"

MARK: The man says, "I've been waiting for you."

ALICE: "I'm here now."

MARK: Silence. They look at each other. The man says, "It's a dark night with no stars. No moon." (ALICE pays no attention.) No moon, I say! Isn't it good? And then? (PAUSE.) Alice! Focus! What next? I'm running out of time. (ALICE inspects the place.)

MARK: Focus! (ALICE tries to speak.) Wait a minute. Don't talk! I got it right here. The man is frantically looking everywhere. The woman stares at him, no expression on her face. No. The man is asleep. The woman stares at him, expressionless. That's better. The man wakes and jumps up. That's it.

ALICE: The man, woman, man, woman. Doesn't sound good. And I don't mean to hurt you, I'm not that kind of a person, you know it. But your play sounds nothing like the one I had started. It'll be a flop. Not at all interesting.

MARK: It will be when I finish it. The man wakes and jumps up... All sweaty? Yes, all sweaty. Why is he sweating? Did he have a nightmare? What woke him up? A sound maybe? The man sees the woman staring at him and says, "Where have you been?" (MARK glances at ALICE, who gestures "It stinks.") The man stands up and says, "Where have you been?", but the woman doesn't answer. She gets up and starts looking for... What are you doing there?

ALICE: I'm looking for my cigarettes. Where are they? (ALICE rummages through the place and searches everywhere.)

MARK: You're not smoking in here.

ALICE: I will if I want to. Do you think it'll be bad for me?

MARK: I try to quit.

ALICE: The man offers the woman a cigarette and she says, "No, thank you. I'm trying to quit."

MARK: (He writes.) The man takes an ivory tobacco can from the inside pocket of his jacket and offers the woman a cigarette and she says "I'm trying to quit."

ALICE: And... and... and... Blah, blah... Too long.

MARK: The man takes an ivory tobacco can from the inside pocket of his jacket. Period. He offers the woman a cigarette. "I'm trying to quit."

ALICE: Quit. By all means. It doesn't do you any good.

MARK: What was I writing? You got me all messed up. That's another scene. Where was I? (MARK looks through his papers.)

ALICE: "His wife doesn't answer. He gets up and starts looking for her."

MARK: Right. (He writes.) The woman is frantically looking around. What is she looking for now? She's turned everything upside down, upset everybody. No. She didn't use to be like that. I've lost it. You got me mixed up again. What is she looking for? I wish I knew what the hell this mysterious woman is looking for in a dark room with no furniture.

ALICE: I wouldn't say that. (She looks around.) Look at this old junk. Where did you find it? Why did you bring it here?

MARK: So what, the room wouldn't have any furniture? Is there any reason to have an empty stage? Nope. Note: Correct the description of room. Too packed with furniture.

ALICE: (She fumbles the antiques.) I never liked old stuff. They make me sad.

MARK: A man enters the dark stage, which is packed with furniture, and looks for a place to sit. Finally, he sits on a chair by the window.

ALICE: I want you to read what you've written so far. Beginning to end. In chronological order.

MARK: Not now. This is my moment of inspiration.

ALICE: Really? And what if suddenly the light went out and everything plunged into deep, impenetrable darkness? (Suddenly, the lights go on and off and it gets dark.)

MARK: What's the matter?

ALICE: Where's your inspiration now?

MARK: Must be some blown fuse.

ALICE: Very prosaic. Unpretentious. Uninspired. You might as well have said: The light of creation is out! Creatures of the world beyond, spirits or ghosts that haunt those who upset the morals, the natural order of things, these are to blame. Whoever is to blame tonight, they shall pay. In this darkness, the truth shall shine above. (ALICE bursts out laughing.)

MARK: What are you laughing at, you silly cow?

ALICE: You're pale from fear. I don't imagine you're one of those who believe in spirits and ghosts? Till I count to... four, the light will come back.

MARK: Four?

ALICE: One, two, three... Are you ready? Four. (The light comes back on.) I haven't lost my touch! Three cheers for me!

MARK: Shall we get on with it? This starts getting on my nerves.

ALICE: You've grown very grumpy, do you know that? You weren't like that.

MARK: Fuck my life – are we going to write anything decent?

ALICE: Listen, I'm warning you. If you keep talking to me like that, I'm out of here. I'm very sensitive. I get hurt. Mark my words.

MARK: (He writes.) The woman says, "Mark my words."

ALICE: That's another scene. OK. The man says, "We've got to leave."

MARK: The woman says, "Go where?"

ALICE: The man starts pacing nervously.

MARK: He's sweating.

ALICE: He's always sweating like a pig. Yuck! I've got a brilliant idea. Just dawned on me. Get a deodorant sponsor. (ALICE bursts into laughter again.)

MARK: He looks into her eyes.

ALICE: She looks into his eyes. A confrontation. They both stand still. One opposite the other. Only one of them will get out alive (RINGTONE.) from in...

MARK: Fuck my life. Who is it now? (MARK looks at the incoming call.)

ALICE: ...there. You interrupted me. I don't like to be interrupted when I speak. I lose my thread. Won't you take it? Someone is looking for you.

MARK: I'll take it when I want to. (Phone ringing for quite some time. The answering machine starts.)

ANSWERING MACHINE: You have reached Mark and Alice Johnson. We are not here right now. Please leave your message and we'll get back to you as soon as possible. BEEP.

ALICE: Haven't you changed this message?

MARK: Never found the time. Where was I? The man keeps looking for…

ALICE: Is this where you stopped?

MARK: I can't figure out what he's looking for. If only I knew. Everything would be easier. All this time, I've been trying to think what this elegant man is doing in this room and what he's so frantically looking for. And you won't lift a finger. As if you're not here.

ALICE: The woman says, "I'm here, I've just arrived. Am I late?"

MARK: I feared you wouldn't come.

ALICE: I'm here now with you. Let's go.

MARK: Where?

ALICE: Don't you trust me?

MARK: The man takes the woman by the hand.

ALICE: Correction. The woman takes the man by the hand and leads the way.

MARK: The man lets himself be driven by fate.

ALICE: Fate?

MARK: The man lets himself be driven by the woman. Where?

ALICE: Don't you remember?

MARK: And the man replies, "I can't remember. I don't remember anything. It's horrible."

ALICE: Although I never criticize other people's works, I have to say I don't like it. Too sappy.

MARK: The man stands in silence, lost in his thoughts. He looks around. Tries to find something familiar. In vain.

ALICE: Thank God you're not the poetic type.

MARK: Suddenly, his eyes fall on... On what? There's nothing interesting in here.

ALICE: Nothing interesting? I will take this personally. (MARK looks at ALICE.)

MARK: He returns home and sees his wife waiting for him. As always. Well done, old boy! Very good! (He writes.) Like every night, when he would come home from work, exhausted. And she would always wait for him with a sweet smile on her face.

ALICE: Too mellow. Not like you. (PAUSE) The more I think of it, the more it stinks. Change it. (She spots a piece of the broken typewriter on the floor. She picks it up.) Immediately. (Shows MARK the piece.) It's a –z-. (ALICE places it together with the other piece of the broken typewriter.)

MARK: I like it and I'll keep it.

ALICE: (To herself.) Not much else to do. (To MARK.) When you ask for somebody's help, you have to take it. Or don't ask at all.

MARK: I'll keep that in mind, thank you.

ALICE: One question for the woman "who's waiting for him with a sweet smile on her face every night." What is a young, beautiful sick woman doing in this place?

MARK: Who said she's sick?

ALICE: I'm wasting my time.

MARK: Where was I?

ALICE: Where were you, Mark? Every night.

MARK: The man says, "I'm here" and the woman says...

ALICE: I feel lonely. I'm with you and I feel so lonely.

MARK: No. That's not what she says. She says, "A warm welcome to my beloved love."

ALICE: "A warm welcome to my beloved love." This is disgusting!

MARK: The man kisses the woman on the cheek and then lifts the time-worn...

ALICE: What a nice word. I haven't heard it for quite some time...

MARK: ...time-worn curtain...

ALICE: He kisses his sick lover on the cheek and then the very next thing that crosses his mind is to lift the curtain? No wonder your career is going to the dogs.

MARK: ...and reveals...

ALICE: (She looks at the bog trunk.) A wonderful trunk. (ALICE goes nearer and tries to open it.)

ALICE: It's stuck. (MARK goes over to help.) It's OK. (ALICE opens it from afar with a movement of her hands.)

ALICE: What's all these? Clothes, accessories, a crystal bowl, masks... (ALICE puts on a lioness' mask.) How do I look?

MARK: Fantastic. Gorgeous. As if you were a creature of the imagination. Now let's get back to reality. And he reveals...

ALICE: "Stay away from me. I'm dangerous. Very dangerous. Grrrr."

MARK: Down, evil kitty. (He yawns.) Good. That's good. Enough.

ALICE: "Beware. I'm dangerous."

MARK: Stop being a child, Alice.

ALICE: "Do you hear what I say? I'm dangerous. I'll jump at you. Grrr."

MARK: The man says (He yawns.) "Why are you looking at me like that? Stay away."

ALICE: The man stares at the woman almost flirtatiously and so does she. A confrontation. Did you write this? They both stand still. One opposite the other.

MARK: What are you looking at? (PAUSE.) I'm talking to you!

ALICE: I'll come onto you. Make you suffer. The man and the woman slowly start walking closer to each other. They move in circles. "The man and the woman slowly start to..."

MARK: (He writes.) Not so fast. I can't take it down... Slower... The man and the woman slowly start walking closer to each other. They move in circles. "The man and the woman slowly start..."

ALICE: Did you write it? Why? D' you think it's good? I find it a cliché. And then, you repeat yourself again and again so many times... I'm tired of being a lioness (ALICE throws the mask down.)

MARK: (Looking into his writings. He yawns.) The man is asleep. The woman is watching him, totally cool. He rises and jumps up. Well. I think we should take it from a little earlier.

ALICE: I thought we were going forward.

MARK: (He writes.) Exhausted after all this search, the man fell asleep on his office couch. The woman says...

ALICE: I'm talking to you. Can't you hear me?

MARK: (He writes.) "I'm talking to you. Can't you hear me?" and covers the man with a blanket.

(MARK's eyes start drooping and slowly he falls asleep on his desk. ALICE spots a piece of the broken typewriter on the floor. She picks it up and places it on the typewriter. Then, after she covers Mark with a blanket, she moves her hand and voila! There is darkness.)

LIGHTS OUT

ACT TWO

(MARK is still sleeping on his desk, in the same position as in the end of ACT ONE, covered with the blanket. The phone rings. He is startled and listens to the ANSWERING MACHINE.)

ANSWERING MACHINE: You have reached Mark and Alice Johnson. We are not here right now. Please leave your message and we'll get back to you as soon as possible. BEEP.

WOMAN'S VOICE: Good evening, Mr. Johnson. It's Fanny again, from the publishing house. This is the third message I've left on your machine. Mr. Adams asked me to remind you that this evening at 18:00 you're invited to talk on the culture TV magazine "All About Art" with Zoe Scoville. You must be at the studio at least an hour earlier. When you get my messages, please call me back. Take care. (MARK watches the machine light twinkle. He presses a button.)

WOMAN'S VOICE: Good morning, Mr. Johnson. It's Fanny, from the publishing house. It's about 10.20... (MARK presses a button.)

WOMAN'SVOICE: Mr. Johnson. This is Fanny. It's 11.15 and Mr. Adams... (MARK presses a button.)

MAN'S VOICE: Mr. Johnson, this is Paul Mathews. From "Art Today." I need your answers for the interview by tomorrow, together with the photos.... (MARK presses a button.)

ANSWERING MACHINE: All messages will be deleted. Please press hashtag to confirm. (MARK presses a button.)

ANSWERING MACHINE: All messages have been deleted.

MARK: Alice? (He looks around. He sees the lioness mask on the floor. He browses through his papers. He reads.) Act Two: The man cries, "Where are you?" in great despair. There's no answer. For quite some time, there is silence. The man cries out louder, "Where are you?"

ALICE: Knock, knock! Look who's here! You didn't think I would leave you alone, not for a minute, did you?

MARK: No. No.

ALICE: You're not getting rid of me so easily. I can see you started writing. What is it?

MARK: Nothing yet.

ALICE: Then, we have plenty of time for exploration. (ALICE almost disappears into the trunk and looks inside. She finds a tamer's suit and puts it on. She takes a whip and hoop in her hands.)

ALICE: Whip. Hoop. I'm a tamer. (ALICE plays with the hoop, she tosses it up in the air and catches it again. She goes through it, puts it around her waist as a hula hoop.) When I was a child, I had this dream, to work in the circus. Don't I look fabulous?

MARK: Be careful with that widget, you may hurt someone. Why don't you go and fool around someplace else?

ALICE: I like it here. I'm a child deep down inside.

MARK: Franklin Jones once said, "You can learn a lot from children. Patience, for instance." Of course, he hadn't met you.

ALICE: Why are you so mean? You know how sensitive I am. I'll get mad at you. I'll punish you...

MARK: Cut the crap and sit down to write. (ALICE gets hold of the whip.)

MARK: Hell, I told you to be careful with that gadget. Alice. I'm warning you.

ALICE: Are you?

MARK: (He writes.) The man says, "Why are you looking at me like this? (ALICE walks towards MARK.) Stay away. Do you hear me? Don't come closer. You'll be sorry".

ALICE: Will I? I think you'll be sorrier.

MARK: The man says, "I'm never sorry. Do not come any closer."

ALICE: You'll regret it. A lot. Mark.

MARK: The man says: "I have nothing to regret."

ALICE: Really?

MARK: Really.

ALICE: Liar. If you don't want to take the blame, you'll pay for it!

MARK: Mmmm... No. This is not what I wanted to write.

ALICE: You don't repent, Mark. That's why you'll suffer.

MARK: Enough with this game.

ALICE: I thought you liked games! Don't tell me you've grown serious now! Old grumpy bastard! You used to play for hours. But not with me. Not with poor little Alice. With other kids.

MARK: This has gone too far.

ALICE: I'll find out about your secret. You'll confess it yourself.

MARK: I have no secrets.

ALICE: Stop underestimating me. You make things worse.

MARK: I'm telling you I have no secrets!

ALICE: Liar. (ALICE gets hold of the whip.) The man says, "This has gone too far." Write it.

MARK: Alice. Alice.

ALICE: I'm not Alice. I'm the tamer. I'll get into your soul, where the beast is sleeping.

MARK: Alice, be serious.

ALICE: I'm Guilt. Erinya. No, no! Even better. I'm Nemesis. That's better, don't you agree? It's a deal, then. I'm your Nemesis.

MARK: Alice.

ALICE: What did I just say? I'm not Alice. (ALICE whips MARK.)

ALICE: On your knees.

MARK: You're nuts.

ALICE: On your knees. Now.

MARK: Alice, pull...

ALICE: Nemesis.

MARK: Nemesis, pull yourself together. (ALICE whips MARK again even harder and he groans with pain.)

ALICE: On your knees. (MARK falls on his knees.)

ALICE: That's my boy. The woman says, "You have to take your share of the blame."

MARK: What's going on?

ALICE: Don't you know?

MARK: Why are you doing this?

ALICE: It's payback time.

MARK: The man says, "Don't come any closer. Stay away from me."

ALICE: Say my name.

MARK: Nemesis.

ALICE: Not this. The other one.

MARK: Alice.

ALICE: I'm not Alice.

MARK: Who are you?

ALICE: The woman says, "Don't you recognize me? Have I changed so much?"

MARK: Who are you? No answer. The man, louder and more desperately, goes on: "Who are you?", while still on his knees. The woman walks around him in circles. The man says, "Who are you? Why are you looking at me like that? Don't come any closer. Do you hear me? Don't come any closer."

ALICE: You're scared.

MARK: The man says, "I'm scared. Who are you?"

ALICE: You? Scared?

MARK: What do you want?

ALICE: You know.

MARK: I don't.

ALICE: Yes, you do.

MARK: I don't know, I swear. The man, still on his knees, says, "I don't know. Tell me what you're looking for." (ALICE goes near MARK.) Stay where you are. Don't come any closer.

ALICE: Mark. My love. Tell me what I want to hear and then puff! I'll be gone. Into the night. Once and for all. Very poetic, ha? Your wish will be granted. You'll be free.

MARK: Cross my heart and hope to die. I don't understand a word you're saying.

ALICE: You don't have a heart, Mark.

MARK: The woman like Guilt or, as the ancient Greeks used to say, Erinya walks around the man in circles.

ALICE: Nemesis.

MARK: Pardon?

ALICE: Not Erinya. Nemesis. We have to call things by their name.

MARK: Nemesis. Right. The woman called Nemesis walks around the man in circles, again and again. The man still on his knees. Begging for his life.

ALICE: I'm looking for you.

MARK: Me? I'm here.

ALICE: No, you aren't.

MARK: The man says, "I'm here. Can't you see me?"

ALICE: Tell me, Mark. What is a beautiful, young, lonely sick woman doing in a dark room full of furniture? In a mountain house far away from everybody? (PAUSE.) You don't speak. You will. You've made mistakes.

MARK: Mistakes? Who? Me?

ALICE: Why don't you ask forgiveness for your mistakes, Mark?

MARK: Stay away from me. Help.

ALICE: Apologize and it will all be fine. This is your salvation.

MARK: Help. (ALICE bursts out laughing.) Are you laughing?

ALICE: You're so funny. You didn't think I'd do anything bad to you, did you? This is a game. For fun.

MARK: Such a laugh!

ALICE: Well, I really enjoyed it. You should have seen your face. You were pissed to death.

MARK: Of course not. Just a bit upset. (ALICE picks up another letter from the broken typewriter. She puts it back on the typewriter.)

ALICE: X. It will soon be complete. Thank God. (ALICE looks around for another letter.)

MARK: With all that nonsense of yours, we've wasted precious time. Where was I? (MARK checks his papers.) The man says...

ALICE: I don't know what the man says, the woman, though, says, "I'm leaving. I'm flying away." (ALICE looks into the trunk, finds fairy wings and puts them on.) How do I look? There's a magic wand somewhere here, too. Wow! Wigs. I've been dreaming to be a fairy ever since I was a child.

MARK: I thought your dream was to work in the circus.

ALICE: I'll turn you into a frog.

MARK: "I would invite you to a mental duel, but I can see you're unarmed."

ALICE: Shakespeare? Quite reasonable. You're colleagues, after all! But, Mark, you shouldn't be talking to me now. You should be croaking.

MARK: Give me a break. (ALICE moves her wand.)

ALICE: Croak.

MARK: Croak, croak.

ALICE: Well done. Now I'll turn you into a cat.

MARK: Meow.

ALICE: It works. Now you're a... koala.

MARK: I don't know what sound the koala makes.

ALICE: Neither do I. A dog.

MARK: Woof.

ALICE: You're a very good and obedient boy. I'm turning you into a man again. If only we could be children forever! Look at me! I'm flying. Well, because I'm a very good fairy, I'll grand you three wishes. Tonight. It's a night without stars. No moon. The secret lovers are hiding. Death is tamed. This night shall reveal dark secrets. Nice, isn't it?

MARK: Splendid.

ALICE: Tonight, all sins can be erased. Forever. Erinyes and Eumenides (The good and the evil spirits – the spirits of guilt and forgiveness.) stroll around hand-in-hand. All wishes come true.

MARK: "Erinyes and Eumenides stroll around hand in hand." Awful. Disgustingly poetic, to say the least.

ALICE: Wait till you hear what follows.

MARK: There's more to it?

ALICE: We haven't started yet. What was I saying?

MARK: Tonight, all wishes will come true.

ALICE: Oh, yes. Sort of. You're not paying enough attention. Let me rephrase, in your way. Tonight, all your wishes will come true. Well, almost all. I'm listening. (PAUSE.) I'm talking to you.

MARK: Me?

ALICE: Your wishes will be granted tonight. Take a step forward. Don't be ashamed. Don't be afraid. I won't hurt you. Or maybe just a little bit. Just kidding. Come. Good. A little closer. Even closer. Good.

MARK: And you will make three of my wishes come true?

ALICE: Didn't we say that tonight all wishes come true and secrets come to light? (MARK is about to speak.) Before you speak, I need to tell you something. In order for your wishes to come true, there is a tiny little weeny mini condition. Have you been nice or naughty all year round?

MARK: You're stepping into Santa Claus' territory.

ALICE: You're right. Still, you have to be totally honest if you want your wishes to come true right away. We don't grant wishes at random. It's fairies' protocol.

MARK: So, you fairies have got a protocol?

ALICE: Of course. Well? Have you been a good boy?

MARK: "The concepts of good and evil are God's preconceptions – said the snake."

ALICE: Nietzsche. Inspired. You're evading the issue, though.

MARK: OK. I was. Nice. All year round.

ALICE: I believe you. You wouldn't lie to me now, would you? Three wishes.

MARK: Let me think.

ALICE: Think? We don't have much time. I know what you want deep down in your heart. I've been watching you for quite some time. I'm your guardian angel.

MARK: I thought you were a fairy.

ALICE: I know what you're thinking. I'm in your mind, my sweet boy. Right?

MARK: Yeah, right. Let me make a wish now.

ALICE: My sweet little boy who never lies, has no secrets and never makes mistakes, I'll tell you which one of your wishes will come true. I will send you to that place you so much long to go.

MARK: Where?

ALICE: The only thing we need is a vehicle to the stars. (ALICE takes one of MARK's papers, folds it into an airplane and tosses it away.) One of my writings, maybe?

MARK: What are you talking about?

ALICE: And we need clothes. An outfit for the high-class, sophisticated-bohemian-artistic type. Rich. Successful. I don't want her to see you in rags. I will dress you up and send you right where you want. Mind you: The spell will last only till midnight. Then, it will be broken and you will be you again. And I will be me again.

MARK: I don't understand.

ALICE: Hold me.

MARK: What's the matter with you?

ALICE: I am your love. The one and only. The great love of your life. Isn't this what you said? I'm the one you held tight when your sweet, beautiful, sick wife was waiting for you all night long – in vain. Don't you remember? I'm the Other woman. You gave me this title. A title of honor. I'll be with you till midnight. Then, you'll get back to her. Like you do every night. And everything will be as it always has been. I'm moving my wand in a cloud of darkness and night will cover us. Come here. Closer. Even closer. Why are you shaking? Are you scared?

MARK: Enough with this game.

ALICE: Too late. Or too early. It's not midnight yet. No one is looking for you.

MARK: I don't want to play anymore.

ALICE: You used to play with me all the time. While she was waiting for you. Her. Now that no one is waiting any longer, why hesitate? Hold me tight. Like you used to. He says, "I'll stay." The woman takes her clothes off and says, "Hold me." (MARK and ALICE embrace.)

ALICE: Tighter.

MARK: He rises and comes closer to the woman.

ALICE: So, he was sitting, wasn't he?

MARK: He's putting his arms around her.

ALICE: The man holds the woman tight. She drives him away from the night. The night of secret lovers.

MARK: Very poetic.

ALICE: Still, very fitting.

MARK: The man says he has to go. He doesn't want to, but he must.

ALICE: Go where?

MARK: To her.

ALICE: Why?

MARK: It's good for my image. The helping husband. The tolerant, the supporting one. It will soon be over. (The square clock strikes twelve.)

ALICE: Listen. Midnight.

MARK: I don't want to go.

ALICE: The deal was till midnight. From now on, you'll be you. And I'll be me.

MARK: The man says, "See you."

ALICE: You bid farewell and leave her. Return to her. As if nothing happened.

MARK: She says, "Goodbye."

ALICE: Too final.

MARK: The man says, "I want to stay here forever." (A snake tail pops under the fairy costume.) What's this?

ALICE: Don't you like me? (ALICE holds him tighter with her snake tail.) Don't you like my tail?

MARK: What's happening?

ALICE: My little snake tail. Don't tell me you don't like it. You'll hurt me. You know how sensitive I am.

MARK: You're squeezing me.

ALICE: Does it hurt?

MARK: It's too tight.

ALICE: Does it hurt?

MARK: I can't breathe.

ALICE: You're not telling me what I want to hear, Mark. Does it hurt?

MARK: Yes. It hurts!

ALICE: Two more wishes. The first took you to the stars. And you found all that you were looking for. You found her. Both of them. All of them. "Whoever loves snakes will be bitten by one and whoever craves for danger, danger will pierce his heart." "The viper might rattle, but it's no goldfinch," "To kill a snake, cut off its head." I'm full of mottos! Now tell me your next wish and I'll make it come true. But only if you've been nice. (MARK tries to break free from the snake's embrace.)

MARK: Let me go.

ALICE: This wish cannot be granted. I can't let you. You haven't been nice. There goes your wish! Lost in the night. You only have one more left. I'll save it for you. You haven't been a nice boy at all, Mark. (MARK still tries to break free.)

MARK: I said let me go.

ALICE: The woman says, "I won't let you. I've warned you. You had to tell me the truth. Now you're mine till midnight. That was the deal."

MARK: OK. You're right. I told some lies. No big deal. That's all.

ALICE: Is it?

MARK: Yes. I swear. I didn't want to hurt her.

ALICE: Who?

MARK: You're hurting me.

ALICE: Who didn't you want to hurt?

MARK: I can't breathe.

ALICE: Which of the two didn't you want to hurt? The sick one? Or the other one? Confess. Apologize!

MARK: It was my fault. I'm sorry. Forgive me. Mercy! (ALICE sets MARK free.)

ALICE: The woman says, "Where are you?" You're not here with me. Once again. (Children's voices are heard from outside, together with a children's nursery song.)

MARK: (In singing mode, taking after the tune of the children.) Eeny, meeny, miny, moe, Catch a mouse by the toe?

ALICE: I'm waiting for you.

MARK: (Singing.) You won't catch me, however much you try. (He stops singing.) I'm well hidden in another woman's arms.

ALICE: Who?

MARK: It doesn't matter. Someone else. They all look so much alike. And every time the night hides me away. (ALICE shakes her wand — the lights are out.)

ALICE: Bloody me! I've got this thing with lights!

MARK: The man says, "It's a dark night with no stars. No moon." You can't find me on a dark night like this.

ALICE: But I can look for you. I'm wearing my coat. I go out at night. It's cold. The woman is weak, pale and desperate. She's childless. "Where are you?" she screams and no one answers. The woman can't take it anymore — she's reached the limits of her existence. Maybe too poetic?

MARK: Quite. Not much into the spirit of the play.

ALICE: Cross it off, then. And I continue. The woman knows. She knows about the other woman. She knows about all the other women. (MARK stumbles on the snake's tail.) Watch it. You're stepping on my tail. You will fall. (MARK falls down.) I warned you.

MARK: I'm crippled!

ALICE: Why can't you be more careful? You stepped on my tail.

MARK: Leave me alone. It hurts.

ALICE: Stop whining. Sit here. (ALICE helps MARK sit on a chair, where the interview papers are forgotten. ALICE takes them in her hands.) This tail is too heavy. And difficult to move around. (ALICE takes off her tail and wings.) The wings, too. I'll take them off. Enough is enough. (ALICE reads MARK's answers.)

MARK: It hurts. Why don't you move that wand of yours to make the pain go away? Can you?

ALICE: Of course I can. I can do everything. But I don't want to!

MARK: What? Why?

ALICE: (She reads.) "As soon as I graduated, I got a full scholarship in Paris. There, I met a student at the School of Fine Arts, Alice. My muse. The woman who stood by me throughout my life, through all my decisions." Just this. A name and the muse. And how supportive I was. Not a single word about my help. About my scripts. My sacrifice. "The truth is – we didn't feel the need to have a family. I guess I can now say we didn't want children, after all. Motherhood and fatherhood are not for everyone. [...] Anyway, it was a joint decision, my wife's and mine. [...] A good reason why we didn't have any children was that I wanted to devote myself to writing." I wanted children. You knew it. How dare you tell all these lies?

MARK: It's all about my image.

ALICE: We sacrificed everything for your public image.

MARK: Forever whining! (MARK strokes his back.) I'm also in pain, but I never moan about it. Shall we go on?

ALICE: You should finish the interview.

MARK: I'll do it later. Work comes first.

ALICE: (She reads.) What are your dreams?

MARK: Pardon?

ALICE: Your dreams, Mr. Famous Writer. What are they? This is the question. Answer it.

MARK: I'd rather we focused on the play. There's not much left.

ALICE: First, you have to answer. My dear friends, the hot issue of the day is: What are the dreams of the great writer Mark Johnson? In order to shed light on this extremely important matter, together with us is a woman who knows it all and sees it all. (ALICE takes the crystal ball in her hands, the one she found in the trunk earlier. She puts a scarf on her head.) Madam...

MARK: Alice. Enough with this childish nonsense. For God's sake, we've got work to do. Alice!

ALICE: I'm not Alice. I'm Madame Morgana. No. Let me think. I've got it right here on the tip of my tongue. Olega. I'm Madame Olega.

MARK: Madame Olega. Very catchy.

ALICE: Merci.

MARK: Very well, Madame Olega, you played enough for today. Let's get down to work.

ALICE: We have hardly begun, you blasphemous man. Now I will see the truth. And so will you. I can see...

MARK: Want some buck? You shouldn't give it for free. À propos, this is a lovely scarf you're wearing. It gives you... How can I put it... something special. Style. Finesse. Elegance. And of course the leftover-from-your-previous-game wand, it is fantastic, too.

ALICE: I'm going to see your past in this crystal bowl. I'm going to see your dreams and your uncertain future in this crystal bowl. I'll have a look into your soul. What you're hiding deep inside. Inside your soul. Into your heart. And mind. I'll also see where she went when she came out that dark night looking for you. Unless you don't want me to. Do you?

MARK: I do.

ALICE: Are you ready to look the truth straight into her eyes?

MARK: Alice, please, enough with this bullshit. Let's write something.

ALICE: The night had pity on us. I can see...

MARK: What? What? I can't wait.

ALICE: I can see you. You're handsome. Young. You have potential. You can do everything. You're writing. You're already famous. Everyone looks up to you. After all these efforts and hard work, at last! You did it. All by yourself? No, still, it's you everyone admires. Everyone loves you. All women are in love with you. They fall into your arms.

MARK: You're so right. Handsome, smart, young. Full of potential. Hell knows what else.

ALICE: It certainly does.

MARK: Anyway, to be fair, Madame Olega, you don't need a magic crystal bowl to see all these.

ALICE: You. You take very good care of her. The one. And Only. Together forever. Till death do you part. The perfect image.

MARK: Yes. She's beautiful, nice and sweet. Very pure. And generous. Patient, with a big heart. I take care of her. Good care. I love her.

ALICE: And her family. They are old money.

MARK: I... These things don't matter to me.

ALICE: Can she forgive?

MARK: She can. (MARK is thinking.) I know she can. She's capable of forgiving everything.

ALICE: A black cloud. It wraps you inside.

MARK: Now you blew it.

ALICE: Stop. Don't talk. I can see... An A.

MARK: Aaaargh.

ALICE: Don't make fun of me. I get hurt. You know how sensitive I am.

MARK: The A. Something is going on with that A. I'm burning to find out.

ALICE: Your sick wife is waiting for you.

MARK: Is she?

ALICE: She's waiting for you. But you're not there.

MARK: Obviously. Since she's waiting.

ALICE: You're not where you should be. Where are you, Mark? (MARK starts to talk.) Don't speak, not just yet. I'll tell you. You're with another woman. The Other woman. One of the others — while your sick, pale, weak, childless wife is waiting for you in your empty house in the mountain.

MARK: Alice, this has gone too far.

ALICE: Your wife, the one and only, your eternal love, the one you praised in all your writings, your inspiration, your MUSE tries to understand why. Why? Since she gave it all up, sacrificed it all, your unborn children, her career, her scripts, her thoughts. Herself. Why were you hiding in the middle of the night in the arms of the other woman.

MARK: Will she understand?

ALICE: What was your wish every day, Mark?

MARK: I didn't have any wish.

ALICE: What were you wishing for, Mark? What was your dream?

MARK: I didn't mean it.

ALICE: Yes, you did. And she knew it. She figured out what you were thinking. What you wished for. What you dreamt of. She knew it. She was pale. Weak. Sick. Alone, Without any children. Without love. Without you. And now she knows. She's a burden. The night didn't hide your thoughts as safely as you hoped for. Because she saw right into your soul. She heard your prayers. She knew you wanted your freedom. And she gave it to you.

MARK: What else do you see?

ALICE: I can see. She's weak. She's cold. Coughing. She's pale. Alone. She staggers. She has a hard time, but gets up. She puts on her coat; she's determined. She wants to set you free. She wants out.

MARK: Wait.

ALICE: She's leaving.

MARK: Wait.

ALICE: She's gone.

MARK: (MARK violently grabs ALICE and shakes her.) Where is she going? Speak. Where?

ALICE: I can't see anymore. The darkness of the soul is too deep. The night you thought a friend now allied with her.

MARK: Where did she go? I won't ask another time.

ALICE: Gone.

MARK: (MARK lets go of ALICE.) I have to find her.

ALICE: You won't find her. You don't deserve it. You're a coward. Besides, why do you want to find her? Isn't that what you wanted? You wished for it every single day. To get lost. To leave her scripts behind and disappear. The woman says, "Your wish is granted. You won't find me. Never again. You're free."

MARK: Come back.

ALICE: You left first, Mark.

MARK: Where are you?

ALICE: And now, Mark. It's punishment day.

MARK: Punishment? What punishment?

ALICE: You still don't get it. Why do you think you've been unable to write for so long?

MARK: No!

ALICE: Why did you call for me? Why did you plead that I would come close to you? Your actions will define your penalty. I'll go away forever. I'm already gone. It's all over, Mark. Face it.

MARK: No. There must be something I can do. There's surely something I can do to make things right. You must help me.

ALICE: You can apologize. A little while ago, you were sure Alice knows how to forgive.

MARK: I'm sorry. I'm sorry. It was my fault. My mistake. You were always right.

ALICE: It's late. I'm going.

MARK: No way. You can't.

ALICE: Yes, I can. I'm going. Leaving you for good.

MARK: First, help me write this play and then you can leave.

ALICE: You still don't get it, do you?

MARK: Get what? (PAUSE.) Get what? (PAUSE.) Alice, I asked you something! (ALICE doesn't speak. She stands still and stares at Mark. The phone rings.)

ALICE: It's your publisher. Won't you take it?

ANSWERING MACHINE: You have reached Mark and Alice Johnson. We are not here right now. Please leave your message and we'll get back to you as soon as possible. BEEP.

WOMAN'S VOICE: Mr. Johnson, it's Fanny again. I'm calling on behalf of Mr. Adams. You didn't show up at the show "All About Art" with Zoe Scoville yesterday... (MARK presses the button and the voice stops immediately.)

MARK: I feel so tired. The man sits on the floor.

ALICE: Someday, you'll have to talk to him. To tell him that you'll never write again. The star of his house has set for ever.

MARK: Forever.

ALICE: I'm going, Mark.

MARK: Go. I'm tired. This illness. So much pain and exhaustion. I didn't ask for it.

ALICE: Me neither.

MARK: It's not my fault. I wasn't to blame for your illness.

ALICE: It's your fault we never had children. You didn't want to. Your career above all.

MARK: And you agreed.

ALICE: Because I loved you. That's why I did everything else. That's why I wrote all your plays and never said anything to anyone. Because I loved you.

MARK: I'm tired of running. Of trying. Of making you feel better. But you never did.

ALICE: It wasn't the illness that tore me apart. It was you. Your betrayal.

MARK: I was tired of being buried in this house. Locked in all the time. I was young. I wanted to live.

ALICE: Me too.

MARK: You were sick. I didn't deserve it. All this hustle. I didn't. I was handsome, smart, gifted. I was a famous writer.

ALICE: I made you famous.

MARK: By myself. I did it all by myself. I got out of the muck by myself. Because I wanted to live.

ALICE: So did I. I wanted to live. With you.

MARK: I wanted to have a good life. I wasn't happy. Your illness devoured it all. It wasn't fair. You shouldn't be sick, I had the right to a good life, didn't I? I was young. And you buried me here alive. By your side. Taking care of you, day and night. Day and night. Every single day. Every single night. You had needs, but so did I. I have needs, too, to have a good life, I have the right, you know? At least you could have died. But no, you clung to life, refusing to let go. You clung to me, sucked my blood like a leech, you ate me alive. You buried me in the muck, in here, in this house. You were worse than my parents. At least they were a couple of uneducated morons. While you. The sophisticated one. You graduated from top schools. You were perfect. Impeccable. Never struggled for anything — why should you? Everything would land on your plate, your golden plate. You were a parasite, that's what you were. I was young, handsome, I had dreams. I wanted to live. You don't know what it's like to have no right to dream. To have no one to talk to. To live with the pigs in the mud. I had struggled so hard with so many sacrifices, so much compromise to get the mud off my skin, once and for all, and there you go and you get sick. I'll never forgive you for that. I hate you. You made me miserable. I hate you with all my heart. Hate you. I was young, handsome, with dreams. Potential. Infinite potential. Now I'm free. I'm free, at last.

ALICE: From me.

MARK: From you. I'm free from you.

ALICE: See? Your wish finally came true.

MARK: I deserved it.

ALICE: (Bitterly.) You did.

MARK: Now let's work.

ALICE: Work? Now? I'm leaving now.

MARK: But our play?

ALICE: Play?

MARK: We have to finish it. You owe me. (ALICE lets out bitter laughter.) Why are you laughing?

ALICE: You have no idea. I'm so sorry for you.

MARK: Sorry?

ALICE: Goodbye. (ALICE starts to leave.)

MARK: No. No. No. Don't go.

ALICE: Good luck with your writing.

MARK: (To himself.) My writing... (To ALICE.) Alice. Don't go. Not yet.

ALICE: The woman says, "You're free now. Out of the muck. All by yourself. And you should now create all by yourself. If you can."

MARK: You must help me.

ALICE: The woman says, "I don't have to do anything anymore. Me. The sophisticated one. The smart one. The high-class girl. The rich and gifted. Who's never struggled for anything. The parasite — all your words. I'm doing you a favor. I'm leaving."

MARK: The man says, "Please. Forgive me."

ALICE: Good luck.

MARK: The man falls down on his knees and begs. Please. Forgive me. Don't leave me. How can I take my horrible thoughts back. All these bitter words I told you?

ALICE: Very poetic. Not much into the spirit of the play.

MARK: I regret. For my actions. I hurt you. Forgive me. Help me. I'm desperate. I can't write.

ALICE: That's why you called me here.

MARK: Forgive me. You have to. If you don't forgive me, I'll never be able to write again. (PAUSE.) I'm alone. I'm suffering. You have to forgive me.

ALICE: I have to go.

MARK: You promised me three wishes. There's one left. I have one final wish.

ALICE: You have a wish?

MARK: To write again. This is what I want. I wish to find again that which I have lost.

ALICE: Mark. You don't have any wishes left. You only have one question to answer: "What are you afraid of?"

MARK: I'm afraid... That I won't write again. That I may roll back into the muck. What about my wish?

ALICE: Poor Mark. You're afraid you'll never write again...You still don't get it. I have no power to grant wishes. It's all in your mind. If you can write, you will. If you can't... I'm out of here.

MARK: No. Wait. Forgive me. This is what I want. I want you to forgive me. I know you can do it.

ALICE: It's late.

MARK: What about me? How can I find myself again? What if I roll back into the muck?

ALICE: The woman says, "It's late. I have to go." The woman says, "Goodbye."

MARK: Won't you forgive me?

ALICE: The woman says, "Goodbye" and leaves. (On her way out, ALICE steps on another letter from the broken typewriter. She picks it up and shows it to MARK.)

ALICE: R. The last piece. (ALICE throws it at MARK.) Catch. (ALICE exits.)

MARK: (He doesn't make it to catch the piece and picks it from the floor.) Won't you forgive me? Don't go, Alice, please forgive me. I don't want to be left alone. I need you. I'm afraid. D' you hear me? I'm afraid I'm still there. In the muck. That I never got away...Even though I peeled off my skin to make it go. Alice. Save me. D' you hear me? (He writes.) The man still on his knees hears the footsteps of the woman as she walks away. Sound of door closing. The man is alone again. Is he still on his knees? (He writes.) He grabs his head. Woe. He screams "No." He screams, "Why me? I'm young, it's not fair." No way. This is corny like hell. The man says, "Won't you forgive me? Don't go. Alice. Forgive me. Can you?" I think I have too many repetitions. (He writes.) The man still on his knees hears the footsteps of the woman as she walks away. Sound of closing door. Silence. Silence. Silence, twice? Lights out. Curtain. No. (He erases and writes again.) Half light. The man is still on his knees. And curtain. Much better. Well. (He writes.) Half-light. The man still on his knees and, while the curtain goes down, he hears footsteps. A woman's footsteps. Her footsteps. The man screams as the curtain comes down, "Won't you forgive me? Please forgive me." (The phone rings. MARK checks the number of the incoming call.) Yes? Good evening, Fanny. I'm waiting. Thank you. [...] Mr. Adams. I know. I didn't go to the show. [...] No, I haven't written the questions either. [...] And I missed the deadline again. I see. [...] I can't blame you... (Children's voices are heard from outside.) But what I'm writing right now will be the best... [...] Maybe if you gave me another chance... [...] Please... Don't you want to rethink about it, I... [...] Wait a minute. It's just a small setback. I have all these ideas... [...] No, don't say that... (MARK leaves the phone down. He's still on his knees, and —)

CURTAIN